ASHLEY REYES

Unmasking Obsession

This novel is entirely a work of fiction. The names, characters and incidents portrayed in it are the work of the author's imagination. Any resemblance to actual persons, living or dead, events or localities is entirely coincidental.

First edition

ISBN: 9798865239703

This book was professionally typeset on Reedsy.
Find out more at reedsy.com

This book is dedicated to every good fucking girl, and to those with dreams of masked men.
I'm sorry, Mom and Dad.

Contents

Trigger Warning

This book is a DARK romance and contains content suitable for adults only. Some of the content in this book may be triggering to some individuals. Including, but not limited to: murder, blood play, mentions of sexual abuse, knife play, drugging, dub-con, stalking, cutting off limbs, anal play, gore, forced orgasms, breath play, mentions of self-harm, praise/degradation kink, mask kink, violence, possessive/obsessive mmc, abuse, CNC, bondage.

Playlist

Ursine Vulpine - Wicked Game
2WEI - Toxic
Bad Omens - Just Pretend
Arankai - Paint It Black
Austin Giorgio - I Put A Spell On You
Bryce Savage - Control
Austin Giorgio - Dangerous Hands
Allistair - Cyanide
Ruelle - Secrets and Lies
Zayde Wolf - New Blood (Reimagined)
Unsecret - Straight For The Kill

Prologue

Before my mom announced that we were moving in with her new husband, I didn't even know she was married. I was fifteen, and like most girls my age, I had a life in our neighborhood. The move meant a new school, new friends, and no more of my crush. We were moving two towns over. It wasn't far, but it wasn't like I could legally drive.

She told me that Jason was a nice man with money. I heard that often, but she never married them. Usually, they slept with her on the side until they got bored of her. She told me about how they were leaving their wives, but I knew they were always lying. I wondered how she managed to keep a man this time around. I never expected to have to move for one of her men. She changed them too fast for me to care about them.

What did this Jason guy see in her anyway?

"He has a seventeen-year-old son. You'll leave him alone, okay? Boys only want one thing from you." I assumed it was the one thing she kept giving them. Why wasn't I allowed to if she gave it up so much?

"So, how'd you meet this one, Carol?" I asked.

Most of the men she met were from dating apps or guys that came into the club she worked at. To them, everything came with a price tag, and I suppose my mom did.

We were packing boxes when she briefed me on what was happening, and hours later, we were on our way to his house. We didn't have many things in our one-bedroom apartment. We couldn't afford much. The smallest U-Haul we could afford was enough to carry all our belongings—most of which were Mom's things she got as gifts from the men she slept with.

"Little smart ass. I'm your mother, so you'll watch your mouth. He came into my work and bought a lap dance. We've been together for a few months now. He's marrying me to help us out. You'll respect him, got it?"

I rolled my eyes at her stern tone. She had never cared to act like a real mother before.

"So, will you still be dancing at the club?" I wondered. If she had a husband now, surely he wouldn't want that. Especially a rich guy who needed a family as a front. Men with families were much more respected. I may have been a teenager, but I wasn't completely naive to how the world worked.

"No. He wants me to find a 'respectable' job. He's going to take care of us, okay, baby? He has money. A lot of it. And power."

She wasn't fucking kidding. When we pulled up to his house, it was larger than any house I had ever seen in person. He had a circular driveway with a fountain in the middle. He had bright green grass and colorful flowers that lined his entire house. His house was a mansion made of gray stone, with two stories and a wrap-around porch.

It was heaven.

"Wow," I said as I gazed up at the house.

"Yeah. Wow indeed. So do everything Jason asks of you and be a good little girl. Good girls get rewarded, Aster." Hearing the words from her made me cringe. I felt too old to be called a "good little girl" by my mother.

He greeted us as we climbed out of the rental van. She ran into his arms with a smile, and he hugged her tightly. But the way he was looking at me over her shoulder gave me the creeps.

"Aster," he said as he approached me, bending down to my height. "It's nice to meet you. Your mom has told me so much about you. Let's get inside." He placed a hand on my lower back as he ushered me inside. I felt bile in my throat waiting to come up. He didn't touch me like a stepfather would.

One of his four housemaids brought me to a room on the second floor. Mom's room was downstairs with him. My room was larger than our entire apartment. Maybe our luck was changing after all. Maybe Jason would be the savior she spent years looking for. Maybe I'd have a better life.

Or maybe it was all an illusion of security.

Then, a smug seventeen-year-old with tattoos walked into my room. My heart thumped, with fear or with excitement, I couldn't tell. For whatever reason, he was shirtless—not that I minded.

"Hello," he said slyly, leaning against the open door frame. "You must be my new *sister*," he said with a smirk, winking at me.

I hated how he said the word like he'd never actually viewed me as one. It was fine by me, though. I never wanted a brother. Especially not one that made me feel this way when I looked at him.

"If you're seventeen, how do you have so many tattoos?" I asked, cocking my head as I looked his toned body up and down. I never truly felt sexual attraction toward another human being until now.

He shrugged and smirked. "My father doesn't care what I do.

It helps to have a fake ID that says I'm nineteen." He winked.

I bit my lip. "Can I get one?"

"Yeah, right. Like you'd need one," he said, his smirk turning into full-blown laughter at my expense.

We were interrupted by the sounds of moaning coming from downstairs. I was used to it from before, with all the other men. Since they were married with wives and children, she often had to bring them over. Sometimes, they bought a hotel room together. Yuck.

"You'll get used to it," he offered with a shrug. "If you even know what that is."

"Of course. I'm fifteen, not stupid," I huffed.

I crossed my arms on my chest and glared at him, hoping he'd go away.

He chuckled. "Not stupid. But you are a virgin," he said, walking toward me. He circled me, me looking up and down before stopping inches in front of my face.

"I am not. How would you even know?" I was, but he didn't need to know that. It wasn't like I had it tattooed on my forehead or something that would announce my status.

He smirked before leaning forward, placing his palms on my cheek, and bringing my body toward his. He smashed his lips against mine, and I melted inside. I had never been kissed before. My first kiss was with my new stepbrother. I was too surprised to kiss back. Once the shock subsided, I pulled myself away and slapped him.

"What the hell are you doing?" I questioned. "You're my new brother." It was wrong.

"Oh, she's feisty. I like that." I went to slap him again, but he caught my wrist in his hand. "I was proving a point. You're a virgin, and you kiss like one. Don't worry; I'll change that eventually. For now, save all your firsts for me. Or else."

Aster

I t had been a month since I heard a peep from my stalker—thirty days with no notes, no flowers on my doorstep, and no immediate fear for my life. I knew why he disappeared but didn't understand why he was back. Preston was still my boyfriend. Since my stalker constantly had his eyes on me, I knew he saw the way Preston had slapped me when he saw a flower in my kitchen. It was in a vase, something I hadn't done, meaning he had come into my house, found a vase, and set a flower there while I was at work.

Preston thought I was seeing someone else. I had a black eye for a week and a half after that. The stalker's last note was left on my pillow, and all it said was *sorry*. The creepiest part wasn't him breaking into my house; it was how he left asters. He knew my name. I'm sure it wasn't hard to find, though.

I spent months wondering what I could've done to catch the attention of a stalker. Where did he see me, and when did his obsession start? Did he follow me for a while before making his move, or did he act imminently? After he appeared, I became more cautious about what I looked like and who I let around me. If Preston wasn't by my side–though he thought I made the stalker up—then my best friend, Briar, was. Much like she was right now.

Before I moved toward the dead flower in front of my door, she walked up the steps, picked it up, and set it in the trash bin by my garage.

"Ignore him, Aster. He's trying to get under your skin."

It was easy for her to say since she didn't have someone making her fear going to the grocery store or even existing in her own house. Her boyfriend, Dex, was the kindest guy I knew and doted on her obnoxiously.

"What if Preston finds out and gets mad? He'll think I'm cheating. *Again.* When I'd never cheat on someone."

"First of all, you need to kick Preston's ass to the curb," she advised, but she knew I wouldn't. I was under the spell of a charming man, and he was the only person I had ever been with. For some reason, I liked the sentiment of my first being my last. "And didn't you say he hasn't spoken to you since your fight last night?"

I gritted my teeth.

It was a sore subject to talk about him ignoring me after he hit me again, which was something I left out of the conversation. The bruise was hidden this time. It was only the third time in our year together, and it was my fault anyway. I was learning to better speak to him to not upset, anger, or annoy him.

"Yeah. Sometimes, he goes off the radar for a few days, but we'll see him at the party tomorrow night." I shrugged, trying to play it off.

Tomorrow was the giant Halloween party we attended every year at one of the frat houses. Hundreds of fellow college students would fill the place by nine at night. There would be a costume contest, a shit ton of alcohol, and a DJ. Briar would do something sweet; I'd do something slutty.

"You said he's ghost face and wants you to dress as...what?"

I sighed. She knew it and wanted to hear me repeat it. I sounded ridiculous. "The slutty-looking girl from the horror movies who always dies first," I reminded her. It was Preston's idea, and I had already agreed to it. My costume didn't involve anything that didn't already exist in my wardrobe. "Can I borrow some of your fake blood, too?"

Briar rolled her eyes. "Only if you let me apply it."

"Duh. I'd fail if I tried myself, but you do it professionally." Briar was the makeup artist for our local haunted house. Tomorrow was one of the nights she had to work and prepare them for the night, but she'd be done by six to get ready with me.

"I'll be here tomorrow at six-thirty to get ready. I'll bring the vodka," Briar reminded me.

"Of course you will. Why else would I keep you around?" I joke.

Briar rolled her eyes and entered my kitchen, opening the fridge and bringing out a box of wine. "I think we need a drink right now, though." She poured some into one of my plastic cups and handed it to me. I didn't have glass cups or wine glasses. I mostly used plastic and paper products—that way, I had no dishes to wash. I chugged the wine she poured in my cup.

"I think so, too. This is becoming a shit show. Like, do I need to move? Get a gun?" I pondered out loud. Briar's brows wiggled.

"Do you think you could really use a gun on someone? Potentially take a life?"

I laughed. "If it's deserved, yeah."

She may have been my best friend, but she had no idea of my past before I moved to Oak Falls for college. She didn't know the violence and gore I saw—often from my own hands—toward myself or others. I had eagerly killed before. Even if others didn't see it that way, I killed a deserving man. They didn't know the truth about him like I did. Briar looked nervous like she didn't know whether to believe me or not.

"I don't do good with blood," she responded quietly. "I don't think I could. I'd freak."

"You'll be surprised what you'd do when it's you or them," I said blankly.

My mind started to wander back to that night. The smell of his cologne, the sound of his voice, and the voice of my mother screaming. The way she...

Briar waving a hand in front of my face brought me back. "Are you okay?" she asked, frowning.

I smiled. "Yeah. Sometimes I get distracted. I'm probably going to throw on a horror movie, then head to bed, 'kay? Text me tomorrow when you're on the way." Horror movies the week leading to Halloween were my tradition, and tonight was my night to watch my favorite. I preferred realistic horror movies to ones that involved monsters or unkillable beings. I liked blood and gore, too, not jump scares.

She nodded her head. "Of course. I can't wait. Dex is going to meet us there at eight. Has Preston said when he's meeting us?"

I shook my head.

"Well, we'll have fun with or without him," she said with a smile, attempting to reassure me.

Preston wouldn't bail on me, no matter what she thought of him. He was obsessed with me and how he was my first and planned to be my last. He was always worried I'd cheat because he struggled with self-esteem and didn't want to lose me. He was very sweet when he wanted to be.

After she left, I threw on the original Scream and passed out on the couch.

When I woke up, another aster sat on my coffee table.

He made an appearance while I slept.

Aster

For the first half of the day, I had classes. I was in my third year of college, and the classes were getting harder. I was lucky I didn't have to worry about money. Therefore, I didn't have to work like most did. My only job was to focus on my studies, even if my best friend was the only one keeping me in line.

I stopped and got a salad on my way home before getting ready. I wanted to keep it light because I didn't want food to absorb my alcohol later on. It was rare that I actually got out and partied since I was focused on my schoolwork. I dreamt of working in marketing and communications one day, no matter how weird people thought it was to have that goal.

I wore pajamas while getting ready, but I had my outfit laid out on the bed—a black lingerie top and a black skirt that the top would tuck into. The top was longer in the front and the back but didn't connect at the bottom. Briar's costume wouldn't take long, so I did my base makeup before she arrived. I decided on a thick black wing, long fake lashes, and deep red lipstick. My blush was a dark raspberry color. The makeup combined was dark, beautiful, and something I'd wear in my everyday style.

As usual, Briar didn't knock when she barged into my house despite knowing I had a stalker putting me on edge. She did, however, announce her presence by screaming, "I'm here, bitch." I could hear her from upstairs with my door shut.

"Up here," I yelled back, but she was already in my doorway.

She held a bottle of vodka in one hand and orange juice in the other. My favorite mix. We had the same taste in alcohol, which saved us money when we'd team up on a bottle.

"The dark colors look so gorgeous with your black hair, especially now that you have the curtain bangs. Your cut and color suit you well, my little gothic queen," she said, bowing before me. I laughed.

"You're not allowed to drink until you throw this fake blood on me," I told her.

"I have it downstairs with my costume. We can go into the tub and throw it on," she advised. I nodded and walked to the bathroom connected to my room. She went downstairs and set down the alcohol, bringing up her bag.

I stood in the bathtub, thankful I had bought clothes for the occasion. They'd be ruined with blood now. Since I'd be the first to die, I'd be bloody. I felt like it added an edge of sexiness to the costume. Or else I was just another girl dressed in lingerie. I curled my hair, which was currently just below my shoulders, with a wide-barrel iron. I looked hot. Preston wouldn't be able to resist me after staying apart for days. I'd say his reaction was part of my reason for the inspiration in my makeup and costume. He always said I was allowed to look slutty because he knew I wasn't. Sometimes, he'd act differently and say I was acting like a slut. Halloween would be fine with him, though. Especially since he'd be with me.

"I'm just going to splatter it all over your clothes with a brush," Briar advised.

She handed me a piece of paper to hold up to my face as an

extra precaution. Then, she splashed the fake blood on my outfit a few times, getting my clothes and chest full of the bright red splatter. It wasn't particularly realistic, but that was probably a good thing. I looked great when I stepped out of the shower and viewed myself in the mirror.

"Thanks, Briar. I love it!" I told her, spinning around to look at myself in the mirror.

If I smiled, I kind of just looked like a serial killer. Hell, I'd make one seriously hot serial killer. I looked good covered in blood. "I wish I was a killer instead. I think I'd look hot carrying a bloody knife."

Briar was already in the other room, changing into her costume, but the door was open so she could hear me.

"Have I mentioned something is wrong with you?" she joked.

I entered the room to a gorgeous Briar in an angel costume. It suited her well. She was angelic while I was sin reincarnate. "You have, but I accept me," I answered.

"I do, too. Maybe you and stalker boy would be good together. I bet he'd kill for you, and your psycho ass would love that," she said. I grinned widely. She knew me too well.

"You're right. I would love that. But he's creepy, leaving asters and coming into my home. I don't even know what he looks like. Besides, I'm happy with Preston," I explained.

"So if Preston killed for you—and, let's say, stalked you—would that be fine?" she asked, sighing. Briar wasn't his biggest fan; she made it known every chance possible.

I thought for a moment. "If the stalker is hot, it might be more okay. Unless he gives me the vibes that he'd kill me."

"Do you trust that a crazy, obsessed stalker *wouldn't* kill you?" she questioned, waggling her brows. I shrugged my shoulders in response. "I need a drink," she said, leaving the room.

"Bring it all up here," I said as she walked out the door.

"Duh," she answered back.

She returned a minute later with two shot glasses. She poured us each a shot, handing me one. She gave me the orange juice, too, since I was the one that needed it more. I immediately needed a chaser; she sometimes didn't even need one.

"To psychotic lovers who will kill for you," she said in her cheers.

I laughed as we clinked our glasses together and then chugged our shots.

"If Dex had the proper motivation, I bet he'd kill for you, too," I pointed out to her.

"Well, of course he would. I mean, look at me," she said, putting her chin on her hands, tilting her head, and batting her eyelashes.

"I think you're worth killing for, babe." I winked.

"I'm going to call for our Uber," she said, pouring another shot and handing it to me. Our town was small, so we had only a few Uber drivers. It would take one at least fifteen minutes to get to us, then another ten to drive to the party. We'd have our drinks finished before the ride arrived. We were fast drinkers. "Thirteen minutes," she said, setting her phone aside.

"We better get to drinking these shots, bitch," I said.

I threw back the one she gave to me, then gave her my shot glass again, waiting for her to fill it. I drank a few sips of orange juice before taking the next shot with her. "And you better dance with me tonight."

We took one more shot before gathering our stuff and heading downstairs to wait for the Uber driver to arrive. We planned to drink more at the party and didn't want to overdo it before eight even hit.

"Our Nissan Altima is here. Let's fucking go, bitch," Briar revved, practically running out of the house. I grabbed my purse with my pocket knife, keys, wallet, and phone, following behind her.

Aster

Our Uber driver was a creep. I didn't grow up here, so I didn't know him, but Briar did. Paul. He couldn't stop staring at us and smiling in the rearview mirror. I was thankful when we arrived at the party. I fled out of the car with Briar, running inside. When Paul took off, I felt relieved. For a few minutes, I wasn't sure he would take us to the party. I thought maybe he'd take us to a secluded cornfield instead since they surrounded the small city.

"Paul has always been strange. He's harmless, though," Briar explained. "Now, let's go get a shot. Dex texted me that he'd meet us by the alcohol."

I followed her into the kitchen, which was loaded with alcohol. There were bottles of hard liquor and a keg of beer. Dex was talking to a group of guys until Briar jumped on him, and they started making out. I scoffed. She quickly gave me up, but I understood. I didn't fuck her; he did. He'd always give her something I couldn't, which automatically made him more appealing.

"Here. A shot," one of Dex's friends—I think named Danny—handed me a shot glass of clear liquid. "It's tequila," he said after I stared at the liquid. I shrugged, chugging the shot. I trusted Dex's friends. It wasn't like they were complete strangers.

"What's up, Aster?" Steve, the party's host, said as he wrapped an arm around my shoulders, pulling me into his body. "Welcome to the Pi Kappa Alpha annual Halloween party. Love the costume." He stared down at my tits, not even bothering to hide where he was looking. I rolled my eyes.

"Hi, Steve," I said, pulling my body away from his. Preston and Dex's friends were constantly hitting on me, and I didn't understand it. They knew I was dating him.

I cleared my throat to get Briar's attention again. She and Dex jumped apart, and she fixed her hair before looking at me with a smile.

"Whoops. Got carried away," she explained.

"Let's play a round of beer pong, babe. Me and Aster against you and your best guy," Briar challenged.

"Hey, Jake, let's go play some beer pong," Dex called out to one of his friends across the kitchen. Jake had two girls at his side and frowned at Dex's request but left them behind.

Dex guided us toward the beer pong table. It was in the backyard. I felt warm, so the rush of chill air from the outside felt incredible on my skin. Though, I almost felt like I wasn't in my own skin.

"We'll give you a head start to be kind," Dex said, winking at Briar. Briar stuck her tongue out in response, like a toddle.

"We're about to kick your asses," I retorted. Even if it was likely a lie. Briar was competitive, but she wasn't exactly good.

Things started okay. We each got one ball in on our first two tries, while Jake was the only one to score against us so far. Things were blurry and in motion through my eyes, but it somehow helped me make better shots. Enough that we ended up winning while they still had three cups left.

"Yes!" Briar cheered, jumping up and down. "That's my best friend." She smiled at her boyfriend. "Sorry, babe."

"All's good as long as you jump on me like that later," he teased. My nose wrinkled in disgust at listening to them.

"Come on. You owe me a dance, and I'm feeling in the mood to dance," I told her, grabbing her hand and leading her toward the main room where the DJ and dance floor were.

The alcohol was starting to hit me violently. Usually, I wouldn't have danced sexually with Briar, but tonight I felt like it. I stood before her, my ass to her front, and we swayed our hips together. Our movements captured the attention of all the men in the room. I smiled at some of the onlookers but kept focused on my dancing with my best friend. Something about my movements felt so freeing, and I felt euphorically happy.

After we danced to a song, my body felt warm, and I decided to stop. I had never felt so warm, alive, and electric. Like every nerve in my body was made of fire, but in a good way.

"Wow, Aster. Where'd those moves come from?" the guy who gave me the shot asked, eyeballing me up and down. I scoffed. The men here were getting on my last nerves. I couldn't wait until Preston showed up and took me away from them. They'd never boldly hit on me with him around, thank fuck.

"Wouldn't you like to know," I said.

"Well, yeah. That's why I asked," he responded, rolling his eyes.

I shook my head and walked away. The room felt overwhelmingly hot, and I was spinning despite standing up.

"Are you okay?" Briar asked when she appeared at my side while I was at the bottom of the stairs.

"Yeah, I'm fine." I'm just going to use the bathroom quickly," I lied. I fled up the stairs before she could say anything else, or one of the guys could catch up.

Aster

—

The frat had communal bathrooms for guests, and some of their rooms had private bathrooms. One of the members let me use his bathroom each year. He went back home for the parties and wouldn't be here. I entered his room and let myself in the bathroom, splashing my face with a bit of cold water to help cool my rising body temperature. Thank fuck for setting powder and spray. My makeup didn't budge, but my body didn't cool off either.

I heard the doorknob jiggle and realized I didn't lock the door. Before I could, a man in a Ghostface mask with a white shirt and a pair of tight-fitting Dickies walked in.

"Preston!" I beamed.

I grabbed his shirt and pulled his body against mine. "I've been waiting for you, baby." I leaned forward and stepped on the tip of my toes, moving the fabric of his mask aside to kiss the base of his neck. Thank fuck for my matte lipstick that didn't transfer, too. I nipped at the skin and sucked for a moment, feeling a level of turned-on that I never had before. Was it the several shots? Seeing him in a mask?

Preston grabbed my hips and lifted me to sit on the bathroom counter. Somehow, his hands on my hips felt more sensual than ever before, their sheer size increasing my heart rate. I wrapped my legs around his waist and pulled his body into mine. His thumb slid down the center of my lips before he wrapped his large hand around my delicate throat, squeezing at the sides. It was unlike Preston, but it meant he was finally listening to what I wanted from him.

I whimpered, and my hips started grinding against his bulge impulsively. "Fuck, just what I asked for. I want to see you be rough," I told him.

His head turned sideways momentarily. His eyes scoured my body. His grip let go of my neck, and I pouted. I was relieved when he moved to unbutton his pants, pulling them down along with his boxers.

I felt an intense desire inside of me with every touch from him. A need that I hadn't felt before. It was like my entire body was being lit on fire but in a good way. Electricity coursed through my veins from simply watching his cock spring free. He placed his hands on my hips and pulled me closer to him, my ass barely hanging off the counter's edge.

He pulled my breasts out of my lingerie top, leaning forward and lifting the mask to take one of my nipples into his mouth while still hiding his face. My hands gripped his large, muscular shoulders. I moaned when he bit down on my nipple; then, he quickly erased the pain by sucking and licking at the sensitive bud. My skirt had pushed up and revealed that I had no underwear on. He looked between us when his cock brushed my bare and exposed pussy.

I could hardly see him with his mask, but I knew he looked at me like he wanted to devour me. The mask got in his way. I didn't understand why he didn't rip it off and eat me right there like I wanted him to. He reached between us and ran his fingers along my slit, rubbing in my wetness before he pulled his hand away.

He took his two fingers which were rubbing me, and placed them in my mouth. I sucked on them. It was something he had never done before. I tasted sweeter than expected, moaning at the gesture's taste and sensuality.

I never thought I'd get turned on by a man forcing his fingers inside my mouth and sucking on my own juices. The thought of it grossed me out before.

With his fingers still in my mouth, he used his free hand to line himself up with my entrance, rub himself along my wetness, and thrust inside me in one powerful motion. He was to the hilt in seconds, and I screamed around his fingers. The sensation of him thrusting inside of me harshly sent tingling sensations throughout my entire body. I was hyper-aware of every touch when his hips would press into mine, and he'd briefly graze my clit. It was almost like lightning kept hitting my clit repeatedly.

He removed his fingers from my mouth, moving that hand between us and circling my clit while pounding into me at a punishing rate. His other hand grabbed my throat and squeezed the sides, careful not to put pressure on my trachea. He was obviously more experienced than I thought because he never brought out this side to me. I asked him to, and he said he felt uncomfortable about it. He must've been researching.

"F-fuck, yes. That feels so fucking good. Rough and hard, just how I want it."

He slowed down his thrusts and angled his hips more, each brutal thrust hitting a spot inside me I didn't know existed. It was like nothing before. Before, sex had felt like a chore. Now, it felt like an awakening throughout my body.

"You're such a good little slut for me," he finally spoke in a deep voice that wasn't like his normal voice. I assumed he was really in character and maybe even using a voice changer like they did in the movies. "So wet, warm, and tight."

His words wrapped around me tighter than the hand on my throat, sending me spiraling into my first orgasm. Often, I didn't even experience an orgasm with Preston. I didn't know words could make me so intensely, but his voice was smooth and sexy in my ear.

"Fuck, fuck, fuck," he groaned, his hips picking up pace again. "It feels so good when you clench around my cock."

"Then make me do it again," I challenged.

"I'm going to make you cum so hard you see stars, then I'm going to bury deep inside of you and give you every ounce of cum I have in my body," he rasped.

Something about that sounded so fucking hot.

His thrusts grew more intense. His fingers continued their relentless attack on my swollen, sensitive clit.

With my legs still wrapped around his body, he lifted me off the counter and moved us to wedge me between him and the door. He pounded into me on the door, his hands holding me up by the ass. I felt one of his hands moving more towards my tight hole back there, and my eyes widened as I looked at him. I'd faint if my fingernails weren't digging into the back of his neck hard enough to draw blood.

"Don't worry, you'll like it," he said. "One day, I will take your ass, too." I guess Preston wasn't as plain as I thought he was. I liked him because he was safe, but now it is borderline dangerous, and I liked that, too.

He inserted a finger inside my ass, thrusting in motion with his hips.

He was right; I liked it. It sent a further tingling up my spine, and I moaned as I threw my head back against the door. His other hand placed small slaps on my cheek, and I moaned louder each time. He hit me until I could see the red marks in the mirror. I loved it more than I ever thought I would. Just like I loved being called his slut. If sex was always like this, I could quickly become one for him.

He inserted another finger with his first, and it only took a few thrusts inside before the edge of my vision started to blur.

"Seeing stars yet?" he asked huskily.

I nodded and bit my lip so hard I tasted the metallic tang of blood. Then, when I let go of my lip, he brought one of his fingers to my lips and soaked up the blood, bringing the finger into his mask and sucking on it. He was doing everything dirty and unexpected, and my throbbing clit enjoyed every second. He shifted his hips again, thrusting savagely into a new spot that worsened my vision. I closed my eyes and let go of his shoulders, swiping my hands under his shirt and clawing at his chest.

"Fuck yeah, fuck, that's the spot. Oh my god," I screamed until I burst again, my thighs shaking and a pleasant, warm sensation spreading throughout my entire body. His hips stilled while I still spasmed.

"Fuck yeah, milk every ounce from my cock. It all belongs to you," he moaned near my ear as I felt warm spurts of cum invade my body. I could vividly feel the pulsing of his cock, too, which was an unfamiliar but pleasant sensation. Once we were finished, we sat in silence with the echoes of our breathing while we tried to catch our breath. He pulled out of me, and his cum started dripping down my thigh, and I really wished I had worn underwear. I didn't know what I was thinking.

"Wash up," Preston said, pointing his masked head toward the shower nearby.

He left the room before I could say anything else, but I took his advice and showered until his cum stopped leaking from me.

I made sure to keep my hair and face dry, though.

When I changed back into my clothes, fixed my hair, and left the bathroom, I was greeted by a duck-taped boy—the boy who gave me the drink earlier. And duct-taped to his mouth was an aster. I stopped dead in my tracks.

My stalker was here. Was he mad that I took a drink from Danny? He was becoming more bold and unhinged.

"Hello, Darling," a smooth, sexy voice of a man that was just inside me said from the corner of a room. It was dark in there—illuminated only by moonlight—and he was a silhouette, but I could still sense his energy. The more he stepped forward, I saw the mask again, but I slowly realized it wasn't Preston wearing it.

Killian

I went into the bathroom with the intention of killing her. I could've killed her many times over the several months I had watched her, but I didn't. I liked watching her too much. I liked watching her fear, her pleasure, and her pain. It took me two years to find her after discovering what she did and learning that she fled the state. I left my father in Oregon to go across the ocean and study in another country, and when I came back, he was gone. When I asked his wife what the fuck happened, she could only say one name. That name made me sick.

I'd come to hate that name and the girl that held it.

Aster.

Her daughter. The girl I was obsessed with.

She killed my father and then abandoned her mother. I had her tracked down and intended to get revenge for my father. I would have if she didn't smell so fucking divine, like Christmas and happiness. It helped that every time I saw her and thought about it, she was vulnerable and hot as fuck. She grew into her body over the years and became more confident than the Aster I knew.

Aster came to my home at fifteen, fresh and innocent in life. Whatever happened to her, she was a changed woman. Her arms were now covered in new tattoos, and her hair and make-up were dark. Back then, she preferred everything on the lighter side, and tattoos confused her. I loved that the darkness inside of her had a way of creeping to the outside.

She definitely didn't look like she belonged with the tall, beefy, dumbass, golden-haired jock she was dating. What could those two even have in common? I didn't think of her as the kind of girl to settle for safety, but I suppose I was proven wrong.

When I first squeezed her throat in the bathroom, I intended to kill her finally. She was consuming me, and it needed to end. But the whimpers she made and how she moved her hips toward me only made me want her more. I needed to taste her finally, but I couldn't stop once I started.

Once we had sex, I knew I was all in. She wouldn't escape me now. I'd shift my way to get revenge for my father. To get answers.

I waited in the room for her to shower and clean herself. Even in the dark, I could see her bright eyes widen at the image before her. Danny, the guy who gave her a drink, with an aster taped to his mouth. I could hear his grumbles through the tape while he pleaded for her to save him. He knew I was in the room; she didn't.

"Hello, Darling," I said, walking into the moonlight illuminating the room. "I brought you a present."

She looked at me and started to realize she wasn't with her precious lover. She was with the devil reincarnate. She backed up toward the bathroom, looking between me and the man tied up on the floor.

"He deserves your wrath. Your *killer* instinct," I taunted. "You only fucked me because he drugged you. Ecstasy. You couldn't resist. But I made it good for you, right?"

She was so still she didn't notice me stalking closer toward her until I was standing in front of her, the back of my hand caressing her cheek.

"What do you want?" she asked quietly, refusing to look in my eyes.

"Revenge. Your tears. Your pain. Your orgasms. Your kisses. You," I said honestly.

She looked at me with glassy, lost eyes. Searching for something inside of me that would tell her who I am. I handed her the pocket knife she had stashed in her purse—a sign of trust. I stole it from her when she was preoccupied in the shower.

"As much as the fake blood looks good on you, you'd look better covered in real blood," I told her, licking my lips. Danny started violently shaking his head.

"How do you know I won't drive this knife into your heart right now?" she asked, brandishing the knife and grazing my cheek with the sharp blade. My dick hardened in my pants, ready to play again. She could kill me right now, and I'd happily die turned on.

"Because minutes ago, I made you scream. I made you orgasm twice. I made you feel incredible. And I gifted you this shitbag who drugged you with the intention of you being alone with him instead."

She turned to the man with wide eyes and tears running down his face. She ripped the tape off his mouth, sending the aster to the floor. She stomped on it. I didn't blame her for coming to hate the flower she shared a name with. I taunted her with them for a long time. I wanted to make her fear me. I hoped she had figured out it was me coming for her, but she never showed any sign that she knew.

"Did you fucking drug me, you shitbag?" she questioned

bitterly.

"What?! No, of course not. You're—you're Dex's friend. I would never. Why would you believe this raging psychopath?" he blurted out quickly. I could hear the nerves in his stutter; hopefully, she could, too. He was pathetic and lying his ass off.

"If your terrible attempt of lying didn't tip me off to the truth, then the electric current running through my body would tell me. Or the fact that I feel like I'm burning alive, but it's fifty degrees out."

While she was distracted, I walked behind her, placing my hands on her hips and pulling her back to my chest. "I've seen what you do to men, Querida," I whispered in her ear. Her head tilted to the opposite side, exposing her sweet, tender flesh to me. I'd bite and kiss her if I weren't in a mask. "It turns me the fuck on to see you like this."

"Killian," she said quietly.

I stiffened. With the mask, I didn't expect her to know who I was. I guess I gave myself away when I spoke Spanish to her, considering I did my studies in Spain while I was away. She pulled away from me as if taken out of my trance, then faced Danny again.

"Do you want to know what I do to men that hurt women, Danny Boy?" she asked him with a wild look in her eyes.

He shook his head like a little bitch, then she leaned forward and slashed his throat before he could spew a bullshit response. I watched as the blood spilled onto the floor, and his body fell over, limp. The blood had splattered onto her, just barely, but it was fucking hot. Thankfully, it was Halloween. No one would question someone being covered in blood.

My dick twitched in my jeans again, and I groaned. She stayed unmoving while she stared at him. She held the knife in the air, and I took it from her before she noticed, and then I held it to her throat from behind.

"You can't kill me, Aster. We're *family*, after all. I want to make you bleed while his blood is fresh on the knife. Turn around, face me, and don't make any sudden or stupid moves."

Aster

I let him take the knife from me in a moment of weakness. I was stunned—not by the act I committed, but by how I'd have to clean it up and take care of a dead body. I fell right into Killian's trap.

I turned around to face Killian. I wasn't fucking stupid. He had the upper hand, and I wouldn't risk anything happening to me. I'd do anything he said. Besides, he witnessed me murder someone. He could take that information somewhere.

He ran the knife's blade along my chest, only slicing into my skin at the end, leaving about an inch cut in my flesh. He pressed the already bloody knife against the wound and collected more blood. He brought it to his white shirt, wiping blood on it. Since I already had the fake splatter of blood, we matched now.

"Where's Preston?" I asked. The ideas running through my head of what Killian had done to Preston terrified me. He did say he was after revenge. Maybe he got it by killing my boyfriend. "And how did you know to find me here and dress in Ghostface?" I wondered.

Killian removed his mask and showed me the smirk on his face. "I haven't just been watching you, darling. I had to watch those around you to get information about you. I can bring you to him if you want."

I gulped.

I had seen a lot of blood but was unsure I'd be prepared to see Preston's. If Killian hurt him, I'd kill him.

"Did you kill him? He didn't do anything to deserve your wrath, Kill."

Killian actually fucking laughed. "Neither did my dad, *Querida*. You just wanted his money. I thought your mother was the gold digger, but I returned on break to learn it was you all along. And then you fucking fled. Now, get on your fucking knees and be a good little slut if you want me to take you to Preston. Then you can find out if I killed him."

I challenged him with eye contact before I gave in and sank to my knees before him. It was better to listen to what the man with the knife said to do. I took a deep breath before fumbling with the button on his pants, pulling them down along with his boxers. His cock sprang free in my face, which was even bigger than it seemed before. I should've realized it wasn't Preston by his size. It was hard to tell when it was inside you instead of in your face.

I wrapped my hand around the base, and my fingers didn't even connect because of how large he was. I leaned forward, softly swirling my tongue around the head and lapping up the salty precum that gathered. I had only done this a few times, but wanted to be good enough for Killian. I didn't know why that thought was in my head. I thought I got over my crush on Killian, and I should have by now, considering I found out he was my stalker.

I ran my tongue along the underside of his cock while his body shuddered. Then, I brought him into my mouth, slowly sucking down his length.

"Fuck, Aster, that's it," he groaned.

I started to suck faster, hollowing out my cheeks to fit him inside of me but not bringing him too deep into my mouth. I'd briefly lick the head or underside when coming up from his length. Since he was long, I moved my hand at the base in sync with my mouth to cover his entire length. He reached down, tangled his fingers in my hair, and pulled at the scalp. I moaned at the feeling, which reverberated along his length. He thrust his hips into my mouth until he hit the back of my throat, and I gagged, feeling spit running down the corners of my mouth.

"Stay still, darling," he said gruffly. "I'm going to fuck your mouth like a good little girl."

I did as he said and stilled my movements.

He started to violently fuck my mouth, pushing to the back of my throat each time, turning me into a gagging, drooling, sweaty mess. Makeup started running down my face. I soon became a blubbering, whimpering mess who could hardly breathe.

"Fuck yeah. I love bringing a serial killer to her knees and watching her pretty little lips around my cock while I fuck her face. Your tears look fucking beautiful," he told me as we locked eyes.

His words should've reminded me who the fuck I was. A woman who often brought men to their knees, then slit their throats. Judge, jury, and executioner. Instead, it made me more determined to please him. Seeing the feral look in his eyes and the mixture of blood on his shirt turned me on.

"Fuuuuck. I'm going to come in your mouth, and you'll drink every fucking drop like a good, grateful slut."

His thrusts grew more erratic, but I hollowed out my cheeks for him and ran my tongue along his length. He moaned, throwing his head back and tugging harder at my hair. Then, he stilled, burying his length in the back of my throat. Cum filled my mouth, the salty flavor dripping down my throat and the sides of my mouth. He pulled out with a popping sound, and I swallowed the taste. I had never done it before, so my willingness shocked me.

He sat before me, only a few inches taller than me now. He brought out the blade, running the tip along my breast before making a small cut just above my nipple. He looked at me with a hunger and desperation I hadn't seen before.

He licked the blood that fell from the wound. Then, he gathered more with a knife. He ran the non-sharp side along the side of my mouth, where cum was overflowing, collecting blood and semen on the blade.

"Lick it, darling," he directed.

He palmed my cheek, his thumb caressing the area before swiping to pick up more dripping cum. He put the thumb in my mouth, and I sucked it clean before he held the blade before me, presenting me with the fluid he instructed me to clean.

I leaned forward, darting my tongue out to clean up the mixture while keeping the sharp end of the blade away from my tongue.

"So beautiful. Fuck, even when I wanted to kill you, I fucking missed you, Aster."

He put the knife in his pocket and shoved me to the ground with his body, pressing his hips into mine as he leaned down and kissed me fervently.

I should've asked him about Preston, but I was dizzy with pleasure when I felt his erection against my thigh and his lips against mine. His tongue ran along my lips and met mine, and I lost myself in our kiss. I had felt nothing like it before. I remembered kissing him years ago, but this was nothing like before. His kiss now was all-consuming.

I was lost in lust as our tongues battled each other in his mouth, and I moaned into the kiss. His kiss tasted like heaven and hell.

"You taste sweeter than I remember," he mumbled, inches from my lips as we worked to catch our breath. "It's unfortunate that I still have to punish you for what you've done, Aster. How should I do that?"

"Hasn't tormenting me, and fucking me under pretense, been enough?" I questioned.

He laughed with a sadistic grin on his face. "I don't mean for what you did before you ran. I tormented you enough for that. I mean for giving yourself to another man when you promised yourself to me."

"W—What?" That was years ago. He couldn't seriously think I would've saved my virginity for him after he left the damn country and quit talking to me. I took it as his hint that he wasn't interested in me. I figured he met a hot Spanish woman and gave up on his stepsister back home.

"You went to Spain!" I argued.

"And you promised yourself to *me*." He propped himself up with one hand, then grabbed the sides of my throat with the other. "Imagine how disappointed I was to finally track you down and see you with him. Fucking him. Telling him you care for him and building a relationship with him. You took from me, and you fucking left. You betrayed me."

He still didn't squeeze hard enough to hurt me, just enough to send pleasure up my spine while my pussy ground against his bare thigh, creating a wet puddle. "Fuck. Then you do that to me and drive me wild. Don't worry, darling. I'll give you what you want."

He removed his hand from my throat. He kicked his boxers and jeans off his ankles and hiked my skirt up. "I'm going to

35

make this hurt, though. That's your punishment. I'm going to ruin all men for you and ruin you for all men," he warned.

Killian

I felt a rush of wetness at my warning. I smirked as I looked at her, knowing she enjoyed my dirty promises. Years ago, I was attracted to her innocence. Now, I was attracted to her filth. The murders, the begging, the way she looked when she choked on my cock.

It was all so fucking beautiful. "Say 'mercy' if it's too much, and I'll stop. Say anything else, and I won't."

She nodded her understanding. I placed a hand on the small of her back and flipped her over so she was on her stomach. "Hands and knees, darling."

She listened and brought herself to her knees, her forearms resting on the floor with her head resting near them. I used my knee to kick her thighs apart, exposing herself to me. I groaned, taking in the sight.

I grabbed the knife from my pants pocket and cut into my palm, just enough to draw a little blood. I smacked her ass with my bloody palm, then rubbed it to mark her with my blood. "I want to fuck you while seeing my blood on you," I told her. "Looks so fucking good."

I leaned down, licked her cheek, and bit and sucked on the skin. I smacked where I just had my mouth and ran my fingers along her exposed slit. "So wet for me." I thrust two curled fingers inside of her, and she leaned forward with the intrusion, moaning at the sudden feeling. I slid my other hand past her thighs and started rubbing her clit. Her body jerked beneath me, and I smirked with satisfaction. I wanted to make her a mess until she begged me for mercy.

"You respond so well to my touch."

"I'd respond the same to anyone's touch," she mumbled.

I smacked her ass so hard that her body swayed. "Don't fucking lie to me. The chemistry has always been there. You just added to how many orgasms I'm going to give you. I was going to stop when you couldn't take it anymore, but now, I'm just going to keep going."

She shook her head. "No, no. I can't. I don't even know if I can orgasm a third time tonight," she said.

I grinned. I drove my fingers into her harder, putting more pressure on her clit. Leaning forward, I bit her ass cheek and then sucked the skin, leaving my mark. I felt her pussy clenching my fingers, and when I added a third, she convulsed around me, falling apart for the third time tonight. Loud moans escaped her mouth, and I was thankful the obnoxious music downstairs drowned her out to anyone who wasn't me. Only I deserved to hear those sweet noises.

"See, you can, and you fucking will," I told her as she fell apart under me, her thighs shaking and her pussy clenching me so tight I couldn't remove my fingers if I wanted to.

"Killian, fuck, that feels so good," she moaned. "Oh God. I—I can't take anymore."

"Too fucking bad. You will."

I removed my hands once her shaking and convulsing subsided. She braced herself again, holding herself up more now that her orgasm had settled. I let her catch her breath for a moment, and when she wasn't expecting it, I lined myself up with her entrance and sank inside her to the hilt. She let out a small scream and a string of curses, bringing a grin to my face.

I grabbed the knife and hid the blade inside so it wasn't out, then I put it in front of Aster's face. "Suck it," I told her. "Now," I said when she seemed hesitant. She put the folded knife into her mouth and sucked. I remained still while watching, not wanting to cause any accident. After a few seconds, I removed the knife and continued my thrusts. I started out slow but deep. My focus was adding a new toy that she wouldn't expect.

I ran the wet knife down her spine, caressing her skin gently. I ran it between her cheeks, stopping outside of her virgin hole. Tonight, I planned to change that. It started with preparing her. I slipped the knife inside, and she tensed.

"Relax and let me in, or it'll hurt more, darling," I encouraged.

Once she relaxed and loosened a bit, I started to thrust the knife in sync with my hips. My free hand held her thigh to hold her in place.

"Oh fuck, holy shit, that feels...so different. So fucking good," she said before moaning more as I pounded into her slowly but deeply. "I—I didn't think that would feel so good," she admitted.

I shifted myself to hover above her back, changing the angle I hit her inside. She screamed before she bit into her arm to conceal her moans.

I smacked her ass again where my bloody, splattered hand print already lay. "Don't try to hide your beautiful sounds. I want to hear them. I want your pain, your sadness, your pleasure. All of it belongs to me. You're all mine. Say it."

My pace increased, but the depth remained the same, bringing my hip to her ass with each powerful thrust that brought me to the hilt. Her moans grew louder at the new angle I hit her, and I knew I hit the spot deep inside that made her feel good.

"I've never felt so full. Fuuuck, don't stop. Please don't fucking stop, Killian."

I smirked, stopping my movements. She let out a frustrated groan, seeing as I did exactly what she told me not to do.

"That's not what I told you to say," I reminded her.

I moved my hips again, faster than before, ready to bring her to another orgasm soon. I kept the knife in her tight hole, thrusting it as far as possible. It would be nothing compared to the size of my cock, but at least she'd be more prepared. I would've used a plug if I had planned any of this out and I wasn't desperate to claim her.

"I'm yours. All yours to do as you please," she said between breathy moans. "Use me. Hurt me. Fuck me. Make me scream."

I reached forward and smacked her pussy, then pinched her clit roughly. She bucked her hips, trying to move away from me, but I wouldn't let her. I held her body close to mine.

"It's too much. I can't," she groaned.

"You can, and you will. Come for me, Querida. I can go all fucking night," I lied. She made my balls tighten the minute I felt her wet juices cover my cock, but I held back. I had meticulous self-control, and I could get hard immediately after. But I was only human and still had limits. "Would telling you how you're my good fucking slut help you come? Your cunt weeps for me. It knows who it fucking belongs to.." I released her clit from my fingers and slapped her pussy a few more times before I felt her walls clenching around me. She buried her face in her arm, sobbing and screaming as she orgasmed for the fourth timet. I wasn't anywhere near done with her.

Aster

When my orgasm faded, Killian removed the knife from inside me, and I felt relieved. His finger earlier was one thing, but the pocket knife was wider. I hated to admit it, but it felt fantastic. Best orgasm of my life so far. The pleasure was mixed with pain from pushing my body past its limits, and I knew we weren't even done. He said he'd punish me. Give me his all until he had nothing left to give or decided I had enough.

I knew he'd go through with his threats.

I almost thought he was finished when he pulled out of me. Of course, he wasn't.

I felt his spit land on my crack and fall toward my tight hole. I wasn't prepared for this. All I had to do was use my safe word, and it would all be over...but I didn't want to. I always knew part of me was dark and fucked up, but Killian was truly showing me how dominant that side of me was.

I heard the flick of the knife. He took my palm and made a stinging cut, then brought it back behind me and wrapped it around his cock. He ran my hand along his length a few times before letting go. "Every part of you belongs to me, including your blood. The perfect lube."

I felt his hand grab my hair and pull my head up, pressing my back to his chest. The blade of my knife was suddenly against my throat, making my entire body tense.

"Every inch of you belongs to me, Aster. Always has," he said.

I was too full of lust to argue. If I was all his, why did he leave? I didn't have time to process my thought before I felt the head of his cock breaching my most intimate area. It was much thicker than a knife. The safe word was on the tip of my tongue, but I didn't use it.

"Relax, or it's going to hurt more," he warned as he slowly started to push inside me inch by inch.

"Hard to relax with a knife to my throat," I pointed out.

"I should end it all right now. Get revenge for my father and end this obsession with you," he growled.

"Can't fuck me if I'm dead," I responded.

My body started to relax and allow him in as he pushed further. It was better to give less resistance and feel less pain. I knew that in the end, I'd enjoy it. I wanted the hurt. Pain reminded me that everything was real.

He chuckled behind me. His hand wrapped around the base of my throat but didn't squeeze. "I'd get your body as long as I want, and you wouldn't be able to reject me."

I gulped, the weight of his words slapping me in the face. I almost thought he might kill me and get it over with.

"I do prefer the warmth of your pussy, though," he whispered in my ear.

He brought the knife to my shoulder and cut into the skin with a sting. I winced, closing my eyes and tilting my head to the opposite side. He leaned down and sucked on the freshly cut skin, and I couldn't help releasing a moan. "Oh shit. Fuck. The pain...the pain feels good," I groaned.

"Remember how good I make you feel when you're thinking

about killing me," he said hoarsely. "Does your precious Preston know you like to get fucked in the ass by your *stepbrother*?" He ran the flat of the knife down my stomach, dragging it downward.

"Former," I corrected. Though, we did fool around and kiss when we were related by marriage. The marriage ended when his father died, making my mom a widow and no longer legally married.

Without warning, he seated himself entirely inside me, and I let out a small scream at the intrusion. Nothing so big had ever been in my ass.

"Oh fuck, fuck, fuck. You're so fucking tight. Your whole body was fucking made for me," he growled into my ear.

I felt the handle of the knife press against my clit. When I looked down, his hand held onto the blade. It was cutting into his palm, but he didn't seem to mind.

"I can't...orgasm again...I can't," I pleaded. The pressure on my clit felt good but also painful.

"This won't even be your last in this room. Certainly not your last for the night," he promised.

He pressed circles into my clit with the knife, going harder than before. I moaned, throwing my head back against his shoulder. The mix of pain and pleasure was becoming unbearable.

He remained seated without moving his hips for a minute, then thrust into me slowly and gently. I thought he was giving me a break, but then he started to pound harder, his fingers squeezing the sides of my throat.

"Once you orgasm again, I'll relent and let you breathe." My eyes widened. What if I couldn't? I'd die? "And if you don't, you'll die being fucked, and you'll like it like the good little slut you are. I'll make use of your corpse, though. Fuck, I wish you could see the way it looks when your ass swallows my cock. So fucking beautiful."

He moved the knife's handle side to side, pressing it harder into my clit. I whimpered, moaning loudly as our bodies were tightly connected. I felt a stinging pain with every rough thrust into me, but pain never felt so fucking delicious. "It hurts so fucking good. Oh, fuck. Don't fucking stop."

"Don't worry, doll. I wouldn't dream of it," he said hoarsely.

I didn't think anything could make me feel better, then he bit into the skin on the back of my neck and sucked, wringing a mewl from me that I hadn't heard before. After having Killian, I wasn't sure I could ever go back or that I'd want to. Hell, I felt the blood from his palm dripping down onto my pussy and thighs, and I wasn't even remotely disturbed like I should have been. I was too wrapped up in my own pleasure and lust. He was bringing me to a brink I never felt before.

The orgasms exhausted me, and he said we weren't done yet.

Once the pleasure started taking over, I ground my hips into the knife's handle, chasing the feeling no matter how it hurt. The pleasure was worth the pain in the end.

"That's right. Look at my good little whore chasing her orgasm. Remember who gives it to you. I bring the pain and the pleasure, and you love every fucking second of it."

His words only added to the shake of my thighs, the clenching of my walls, and the loud moans I let out as I fell apart in his arms from his knife. He dropped the knife and switched to aggressively rubbing my clit with his palm, inserting two fingers into my pussy while he kept pounding into my ass. I died and went to heaven, and the devil was with me, wringing every bit of pleasure from me.

When the orgasm washed over me, I felt a rush of warmth

throughout my body, a pressure building in my lower abdomen. While screaming from pleasure and pain, I felt myself squirting on his hand for the first time in my life. The liquid flowed and made a mess everywhere. I felt it on my thighs and his hand. I thought the action would turn him off, but he groaned and fucked me with his fingers harder.

I threw my head back against his shoulder and screamed his name, my whole body shaking as I exploded with intense pleasure I had never felt before. My hand reached around and tugged on a chunk of his beautiful, fluffy black hair.

"Fuck, yes, squirt for me, doll. So fucking hot. So beautiful as you fall apart." He took his hand away from the base of my throat, grabbing my hips as he pulled his hand out of my pussy and thrust harder into my backside. "I love how dirty I make you. How I ruin you."

I felt dirty, alright. My makeup was running down my face, my hair was a tangled mess, and I had bruises from his roughness forming all over my body.

When the feeling subsided, my body was spent. I was ready to pass out, dizzy from pleasure and reeling from pain. He pushed me on the ground so my stomach was against the floor, and my face smashed into it as well. He placed himself against me, my back flush against his stomach as he ravaged me.

"Too bad I'm not done with you yet. I'll let you rest while I continue to take you until I've decided I'm ready."

He sat up on his knees, placing his hand on the back of my head and gripping my hair, holding it harshly in his fingers as he pressed my cheek into the floor. I bit my lip to hold back the urge to beg him for mercy. He'd be too satisfied.

"Spread your fucking cheeks for me," he demanded.

I reached behind me and did as he asked. I felt him sink deeper into me, which I didn't think was possible.

"I can't take much more," I pleaded, not caring how pathetic I sounded.

"You can take exactly what I give you, darling. Beg me. Plead with me. Your cries turn me on so fucking much. Maybe I'll finish and let you go."

I already had tears streaming down my face from all the feelings. "Please, Killian. Please let me go. It hurts. Give me all your cum. Fill me with your cum, then let me go. I'll return to that party, dripping your cum down my thighs. Everyone will know I belong to you. I can't take it anymore, please," I sobbed.

Each time I pleaded, he thrust harder into me, his pace growing erratic. On my last plea, he stilled deep inside me, and I felt him throbbing as he released inside me. Even when he stood, I lay there, catching my breath against the hardwood floor.

Killian

Even I was exhausted after that brutal fuck. I imagined it was much worse for her. She looked like she didn't want to move for weeks. I encouraged her by picking her dead weight up. I adjusted her skirt before setting her down on some fucker's bed, where cum and blood would leak and stain. He'd have no way to know the culprit or if the blood was real. It was a Halloween party, after all. Drunk kids stumbled into random rooms all of the time.

"What are you doing with that body?" she asked, looking down at a very dead Danny.

"Don't worry about it, love. I'll take care of it and the bloody mess," I said. "Come. Let's go clean up a bit; then I'll bring you to Preston if you still want."

She nodded, and I lifted her, carrying her into the bathroom and setting her down on the counter. The setting was very familiar. I smirked, thinking about what we did here not long ago when she cemented that she was *mine.* I told her when we first met that she belonged to me. She became my obsession, and it never went away.

Her sweet, wide, brown eyes. Her long, dark hair always gave her a dark aura that felt like temptation and sin. When I first met her, she wore blood-red lipstick, which sparked my need to see her bleed. Her lashes were naturally long, and she could bring a man to their knees when she batted them.

She was perfect—everything I wanted. I shouldn't have let my dad push me to study in Spain. It was his dream, not mine.

A primal need overtook me. I placed my hands on her face and stood at the edge of the counter, bringing her face to mine and smashing our lips together. She tasted divine, like a dream. Father told me I couldn't have her when we lived together, but it didn't stop us from fooling around before I left.

Sometimes, I wondered if he knew and sent me to Spain as a punishment.

She whimpered against my lips, and I groaned into our kiss. My tongue pushed into her mouth and lazily danced with hers. I pulled away before I got too distracted to stop. I put her through enough, even if I was punishing her.

I found a towel in the closet and wet part of it, then sank to my knees in front of her. I wiped down the blood and cum dripping from her and seeping onto the counter. I hated to see it gone, but I had plans to replace it soon in a more exciting way.

I brought her down from the counter and turned her around, having her brace herself with her palms on the counter.

"I just have to clean back here," I told her when she seemed hesitant.

I lifted her skirt to wipe away the remnants between her cheeks, and the sight made me hard again. It was this deep-rooted need to claim her for everyone to see. But then my eyes stopped at something else—scars.

"What happened here?" I asked, running my fingers along the raised scars on her inner thigh. I don't know how I didn't notice them earlier. I knew they were fresh because I had been buried between her thighs several times when she lived with me.

"Don't worry about it," she mumbled.

"Did you hurt yourself, doll?" I asked, looking up at her and kissing gently around the scars.

She nodded her head. I bit down on the skin, and she winced.

"No more. Only I can make you bleed. Only I can cause you pain and break your skin."

I fixed her skirt and opened the bathroom door. I grabbed my mask to throw it back on so no one would know who I was.

"I need to fix my hair and makeup."

I shook my head, chuckling. "Nope. Let's go."

"Preston will kill me," she argued, standing in place and refusing to move.

"Do you say that because you actually believe he'll harm you?" I asked, stepping closer toward her. "Because I will cut off the fingers of any man that touches you wrong, the tongue of any man who speaks to you wrong, and the eyes of any man who looks at you wrong. You're under my protection now. I will not let him harm you."

She sighed. "He's...he's my boyfriend, though. You're not. You had your fun; you punished me. You don't want to protect me, Kill. You want to end me. You talked about wanting to kill me this entire night so far."

I clenched my fists at my side. "Hell no, he's not your fucking boyfriend. You're mine. You can't get rid of me. And I don't care about punishing you for what you did anymore. You're forgiven," I growled, my fists clenching at my sides. She wouldn't get away that easily.

She scoffed. "What makes you think I need to be forgiven?" she said, her head tilting.

"You killed my fucking father, Aster. Your fucking stepdad. The man who was helping to raise you. He took your dirty-ass, gold-digging mother from that trash club. He cared about you. All you wanted was fucking money to live out your life without your parents. Here I am in person, not sending the cops after you and accepting you. Would Preston if he found out everything you did?"

She grabbed a knife from the hem of her skirt. It was different than the one she had before. She pushed me against the door with her arm at the base of my throat and her other arm brandishing the knife against my throat. She still had a fight in her. It turned me the fuck on. I couldn't help but smile, which she couldn't see due to my mask.

"Did you ever consider that I didn't need your forgiveness or punishment? That you'll need mine? My *stepdaddy*, as you like to call him, started to touch me the moment you left. I was stuck with them. He promised to take my virginity or sell me if I didn't give it to him freely. So, when the time came to collect, I slit his fucking throat instead. Before that, I stuck to slitting the throats of men like him. Men who would easily buy my virginity. I took that money instead and left them for dead."

I flinched when she moved the knife. I thought she'd stab me, but she stabbed the door—inches from my head.

"No...no, that can't be right. He called me the week before he died. He said he chose to take me out of the will and put you in my place. He was leaving you everything. You killed him for that money because you're a serial killer. I sensed that darkness in you when I met you. Then, I hacked your accounts to figure out you met all those dead guys before they died. If you're so innocent in this, why did your mother keep saying your name when I asked her what the fuck happened?"

She huffed, and it turned into a chuckle. "My fucking *mom*? Do you know why your father took her off the street? Because she

50

had a virgin daughter. My mom cried because she got nothing from him. He left it all to me. And if you went into his bank accounts, you'd see I didn't fucking touch anything. He set me up for you to believe that about me."

I tried to process everything she said, but it was hard. Everything I knew felt like a lie now. I had made the wrong person pay. I hurt her when I didn't need to. I hurt her for my pleasure. And worse, I didn't regret it. I loved every second of seeing her fall apart.

"Don't, Kill. Don't feel bad for what you did in there, okay? You made that choice. I chose not to stop it. Now, bring me to Preston. Whether or not I stay with him will be my choice and mine alone. He loves me. You don't." She took her knife and placed it back in her skirt holster.

I couldn't believe she still wanted to see that piece of shit. I walked her out of the bathroom and opened the door to the party. The hall was empty since everyone was downstairs at the raging, loud party.

I lightly pushed her into the wall, towering over her with my body and pinning her with my arms on either side of her head. "Love is weak and basic. People fall in and out of love all of the time. And you didn't say you love him, darling. You said he loves you." I leaned closer toward her, inches from her ear now. "I won't say I love you, Aster. It's overrated. It goes past love. I'm obsessed with you. I crave you. I need you. I hunted you down for years to find you again, and I won't let you go. If I have to say I love you to keep you, I'll tell you every fucking day, but you know it goes beyond that. I would kill for you. I have killed for you. I'd let you keep killing just to keep you satiated. I'd kill everyone on this goddamn planet if it meant having *you*."

I pulled away from her and watched as she stood there,

breathlessly panting. I held her hand and brought her down the hall to the room all the way at the end.

"Why are we at another room?" she asked.

We heard moans coming from in the room.

I opened the door with a kick, revealing a naked Preston fucking some blonde bitch while in missionary. He was lame as shit. Too basic for my dark Aster.

"You've got to be fucking kidding me," she said, fuming.

Preston turned to acknowledge our presence, and his eyes widened. He jumped from the bed like she wouldn't notice what he was doing.

"You're literally at the same party, cheating on me?" She stepped closer toward him.

The blonde girl grabbed her clothes and fled the room. I didn't blame her for not wanting to participate in the drama. She thought she was saving him by fucking me. That I had him tied up somewhere, ready to kill him. He had been with this girl for some time now. I needed her to see. I should've brought her sooner, but I was having too much fun playing with my toy.

"It's bad enough you hit me. I was willing to see past it and give you another chance. I knew I could change my attitude and make it better. But you're fucking some girl at the party you were supposed to meet me at!" Aster furiously shouted.

Preston threw on his boxers and pants in a hurry. "Wait, Aster, please. It wasn't what it looked like," he pathetically pleaded. It looked like he had his fucking dick in her. And he did. "Wait... who the fuck is this guy? Why do you look like you just got fucked? And all these fucking cuts? Jesus Christ. You even smell like sex. Are you fucking serious right now? You fucking whore. I knew you were a whore," he seethed, stepping into Aster's space.

He grabbed her wrist harshly, tugging her toward him. "Was it fucking worth it? Because we're done."

"It was worth it because at least I got to orgasm," she told him.

Then, he sealed his fate. He slapped her and threw her against the wall.

I intervened, stepping before her and pushing him down to the ground.

"Don't you dare touch her. I'll end your life right now, Pretty Boy."

"You two have at it. I'm returning to the party; I will drink and dance with my best friend. Then, I will go home an hour from now because I'm exhausted. Preston, don't you *ever* talk to me again. I should've cut your hand off the first time you hit me. I shouldn't have become accustomed to abuse because of one man."

Her last line hurt. My father did that to her, and I wasn't around to stop it. I wasn't around when she needed me most. But I'd be here now. I'd make it up to her, starting now.

I let her walk out the door while ensuring her precious Preston stayed on the ground until I could care for him.

"Wh—what are you going to do with me?" he pathetically asked, his face falling when he realized we were alone now. "My father can pay you if you leave me alone. Aster's not worth it, dude." I wish he could've seen the grin on my face. I wished he could see the way his pathetic pleases satisfied me.

"Aster is worth more than anything, and you're the fucking idiot who ruined it all. Now, you'll pay for taking and touching what's mine."

Aster

I went to the bathroom I was just in before going back downstairs. I wiped away the makeup under my eyes and brushed through my hair as best as possible with my fingers. It was still obvious what happened to me. The cuts looked worse than they felt. I didn't want to hear shit about them, so I grabbed a hoodie from the closet and threw it on. I didn't need to look hot anymore anyway. I have attracted too much attention already.

Returning to the party, I immediately poured myself a shot of vodka. Then another, and another. Briar found me before I could go looking for her. She threw her arms around me from behind. If it wasn't for her slender frame and the smell of vanilla, I might've thought she was Killian.

"Oh my God, Aster. Where have you been? I've been worried." She looked me up and down, then cocked a brow. "Oh. You must've found Preston because you look like you got ravaged," she teased.

I smiled. "Well, kind of. It's a long story. Let's just go dance." She shrugged her shoulders and followed me to the makeshift dance floor. She waved at Dex as he sat on a nearby couch watching us.

At first, we kept it tame. My arms were loosely on her

shoulders as we danced to the music, some Halloween-themed remix of a pop song that strangely worked.

"So, why the sweater? It's warm in here." I felt warmth creep to my cheeks at her question. "Oh my God, you're blushing!"

"Shh!" I told her. "Keep it down. I have a bunch of hickeys, okay? I didn't want to be seen." Lying to my best friend was too easy when it should've been hard. But it was better than telling her that I was covered in cuts, bruises, and blood. It was bad enough that I had to worry about cum potentially dripping from my thigh, especially while moving to the music. Briar was fragile. She wouldn't be able to handle the darkness of my story.

"So hot. I sometimes wish Dex wasn't so boring in bed. Too tame. Missionary, all the time." Briar was definitely drunk, spilling her soul to me. She usually kept quiet about sexual matters, thankfully. I had to see Dex way too much to feel comfortable hearing about their sex life, but it explained why she asked about mine so much.

"Tell him what you want. Go after it," I encouraged.

"Ugh, but it's me. What if he's not interested?"

When I saw a Ghostface appear at the top of the stairs, I somehow knew his eyes immediately found me in the crowd. He was staring now. The hand he cut with the knife while fucking me was wrapped now. I turned myself around to start grinding my ass against Briar's hips.

"Oh, that's Preston! No wonder you're getting like this. And the drinking," she said.

"Girl, you need to tell Dex what you want. Go for whatever you want in life, always. A college relationship isn't necessarily going to last forever, and that's okay. If you don't, you'll resent him later for not understanding your needs."

I understood because Killian understood mine before I did.

Before I knew the darkness was deeper ingrained in me than I thought.

"You're right," she said.

Then, she left me swaying my hips alone. She stalked over to the couch like a hungry lion watching their prey and sat in Dex's lap with her knees propping her up on either side of him. *Go Briar.*

I sighed. I stopped dancing and turned to face the staircase, but he was gone. I frowned. Was he done with me now? Would he leave me alone forever? Did I want that?

I felt hands on my hips, but I heard Killian's voice in my ear before I could slap the culprit.

"I was just starting to enjoy the show."

"You won't cut her fingers off for touching me?" I asked, starting to grind my hips again. I could feel his erection growing on my ass, his fingers digging deeper into my hips.

"She's allowed. She has no sexual attraction to you and is your best friend."

"Yes, Sir," I responded sarcastically.

I was used to Preston trying to control me in an abusive way. With Killian, it felt more protective.

"Don't call me that unless you mean it. Sir or master will do." His right hand traveled down my hip and squeezed my ass cheek. I let out a feral moan, and he clasped his hand over my mouth.

"No one gets to hear those sounds besides me, doll." His hand that covered my mouth slid down sensually, landing at the base of my neck and squeezing between his thumb and pointer finger.

"Such a whore for me. I bet you're already wet." I felt his other hand travel between us, sneaking up the back of my skirt and running a finger through my slit. He groaned in my ear.

"There are people around us," I pointed out.

"And you're too drunk and horny to care," he argued.

I shrugged. I couldn't disagree. I was often open about my body and sexuality until girls started calling me a slut for it, even when I was a virgin. They were jealous when Preston chose to date me. He had fucked dozens of girls before me and was seen as cool, but I was the whore because he was dating me.

"What did you do with Preston, anyway?" I questioned.

"Don't worry about it," he said with a raspy voice that sent bolts of electricity down my clit.

"And what happened to the dead weight?" I asked, batting my eyelashes at him. I wanted him to give me the information, not treat me like I was too fragile.

"Don't worry about that...I've got a plan. They're going to find Danny's body, and they're going to find your knife, but it's going to have Preston's fingerprints."

I turned around to face him, slinking my arms around his neck and pulling him toward me. If he weren't wearing the mask, I'd kiss him. I guess a part of me felt thankful that he was. Drunk Aster wanted to make bad decisions. Drunk Aster liked to hear that he was framing her ex.

"I want you to chase me while you wear that mask, then ravish me. Please."

He chuckled. "We can make that happen soon."

I looked over to see Briar leaving Dex's lap and walking toward me again. I turned my body around to face her, and she was all smiles.

"We're going to get pizza slices at the place open all night. Want to join us? Preston can come, too!" Excitement radiated off her in waves.

My best friend was the ray of sunshine to my cloudy heart. I looked back and realized Preston had disappeared shortly after

Briar disappeared. This time, maybe he'd truly leave me alone. I could leave the party with Briar right now, and then he'd be gone. Did I want that? I wasn't sure.

"Yeah, let's go," I said.

I walked with Dex and Briar out of the party, looking behind me to ensure no one followed. Killian probably had to take care of Preston, anyway. Whatever he was doing, I didn't care. Killian gave me something Preston never could and opened up my world, heart, and eyes. If Killian didn't hurt him in my honor, I would.

The open late New York-style pizza place was only a few blocks away. It was a beautiful but chilly walk.

"Where'd you go tonight, Aster?" Dex asked.

I felt the warmth travel to my cheeks.

"She's blushing again! Cute. She ran off with Preston. Where is he?" Briar responded for me.

"I don't know. He was busy, I think." It wasn't a lie.

The person she thought was Preston happened to be Killian, though. He disappeared when Briar walked up, probably not wanting to pretend to be Preston to my friends. One day, I'd have to tell her the truth. I'd have to explain that Preston and I broke up. I could probably leave out Killian being my stepbrother whose dad I murdered.

"I can't believe that was our last college Halloween party together," Briar pointed out with a frown.

"I know. I hope wherever we end up, years down the line, we're together."

Briar had years left of schooling to be a lawyer; mine would be done in May. I'd have my degree and enter the workforce.

One thing I'd miss about this town was the pizza spot. Once I moved home and got rid of my bitch of a mother, I'd go find a home somewhere, but I wouldn't return here.

"Did you decide where you want to go for law school?" I asked her.

"I think I'm going to go with Harvard. Maybe you can end up in Boston for work!" she said ecstatically.

Being from the Pacific Northwest, I didn't know much about Boston. I only knew that people there had fascinating accents.

We approached the pizza place, and I stared at all the options wide-eyed. College kids in costumes filled the place.

"No matter where she goes, I'm going with her," Dex says, wrapping his arm around her waist and pulling her close.

I'd miss having that kind of cuteness with Preston, but at the same time, I never liked the cute public displays of affection. I guess I always secretly wanted someone to treat me like Killian did. Truthfully, I think he ruined me when he first kissed me. I knew I wanted him. There wouldn't have been any other options for me if he hadn't run off to Spain and never talked to me again.

The chime of the door rang behind us, and something called for me to turn around. When I did, I spotted a maskless Killian with a devilish smirk on his face.

"Oh, fuck," I mumbled.

Briar turned to face me. "What's wrong?"

"Hello, *Sister*."

Killian

Aster's fluster at my nickname had me chuckling. Her cheeks were red and warm, and she was trying to hide her face in her hoodie.

"*Former* sister," she corrected.

"You left that party so fast I had to run after you to find you here. Weren't going to say goodbye?" I teased, tilting my head. Her friend—the girl—was giving me a strange look.

"Was hoping you'd take the hint," she responded.

"Wait, I didn't see you at the party," the girl with her said. Aster was probably unaware that I knew who Briar was, but I knew everything about the life she built for herself.

"I was in a mask," I said nonchalantly.

Briar wasn't as dumb as she looked. Her eyes widened before a blush crept over her face. She realized what I was implying. She was wasted, so there was a chance she'd forget by morning.

Aster turned away and went to order food, but I cut ahead of her. "Two pepperoni slices and two drinks. Throw in some of those garlic knots, too," I ordered.

She scoffed, crossing her arms as we stepped aside to let others order. "What if I didn't want pepperoni?"

"Don't be silly. It's your favorite kind," I responded. "I'm going to go get us a table," I announced.

I took the plastic cup I gave her and poured us both Cokes. Her favorite soft drink. I grabbed a corner booth away from the other students and set her drink down on the table next to me. She slid right in and glared at me.

"What are you doing here?" she whispered.

Her friends were still ordering their pizza, unable to keep their hands off each other.

"Getting my girl food and ensuring she gets home safely," I answered. Did she think she'd get off that easy? She knows I know where she lives, anyway. "Plus, I texted a few times with no response. You'll learn to respond to me."

"I didn't get a text. Besides, you ignored me for years when I tried to contact you. You treated me like I was nothing."

"Ignored you? You ignored *me*." I took her phone, determined to get to the bottom of it. I typed in my contact information and looked me up, chuckling when I got my answer. I shoved her phone back at her. "You have me blocked. Of course, you do." I watched as she unblocked me, then I texted her to test it out.

I'm going to punish you for that later. Her eyes widened when she read it, redness taking over her cheeks. Then, she set her phone face down at the table.

"I swear, I didn't do that," she said before biting into her pizza. "I tried to contact you for so long. I thought you gave up on me."

I bit into my pizza and chomped it down angrily, earning stares from her friends.

"Is he okay?" Briar asked as if I wasn't there.

My fucking father was the only one to blame for our mis-communication. He must've taken her phone and blocked my number. I believed Aster. We had too strong of a connection for her to ignore me for years. Though she did run and hide in a small town, I suppose that was from my father, not me.

"Yeah. He's just bitter I left the party with ya'll instead of him," she said, covering for me. I was staring into the distance in a fit of rage, ready to strangle my old man if he wasn't already fucking dead. I owed Aster. I owed her so much at this point. I'd never be able to make up for everything.

"I didn't know Aster had a brother," Briar said, catching my attention. "What's your name?"

"He's not my brother anymore. We didn't even know each other long, so brother is a bit of an exaggeration," Aster corrected.

"Yeah, I suppose it's weird to call someone you fucked all night your brother," Briar said. I liked her.

Aster shoved her face into the palms of her hands.

I grinned. "My name is Killian. I'm surprised she didn't talk about me. I told everyone about my dear sister at home, whom I missed so much." I loved flustering her by calling her sister, especially when her friends had an idea of what happened between us.

"Now that I think about it...she's hardly talked about her family at all," Briar interjected, her head tilted and her eyes deep in thought.

"We didn't grow up with the best role models, even though we grew up separate," I answered.

"Aster can totally speak for herself," Aster said, rolling her eyes.

"So, Killian. Are you staying for a while?" Briar's boyfriend, Dex, asked. He seemed nervous around me, like he thought I'd jump across the table and kill him out of nowhere. Maybe he felt threatened in a way, or maybe he felt suspiciously protective of Aster. I'd assess that later.

"I'm not letting Aster out of my sight again," I answered

honestly.

It didn't matter if she wanted me there or not. If I had to keep watching from afar, I would.

Aster groaned while Briar chuckled.

"Be careful, she's got a stalker out there," Dex warned.

I bit the inside of my cheeks to keep from smiling and giving myself away. I didn't need to be careful of Aster's stalker; her friends needed to be careful of me. I'd do anything for her. Anything in the world she asked would be hers. Murder? Fine. Dog? Cool. Child? Tomorrow. *Anything.*

"Killian knows all about stalkers," Aster teased as she finally finished her slice of pizza. I had finished mine minutes ago despite having a conversation.

I grabbed Aster's thigh and squeezed, giving her friends a smile. "Yeah. I studied psychology," I lied. Aster didn't know what she was in for when we returned to her place, but she sure was making it worse for herself.

Tonight would be the first time I would be there while she was awake and knowing.

Something bummed me out about that thought.

"It's been real nice to get to know you guys, but I should get this drunken mess home," I said, standing up from the booth and bringing Aster with me by the wrists.

"But I like my friends," Aster pouted.

"Go have fun, kids." Briar winked. "I'll see you at campus Monday."

Aster

I should've expected Killian to show up, but his showing up meant he wouldn't hide himself anymore. Instead of stalking me from a distance, he would try to be an active part of my life. Something I wasn't sure I was ready for. All our previous problems may have been created by his father instead of him, but we still had a lot to sort out after years apart.

He shocked me on the walk home when he took my hand in his, interlacing our fingers. He didn't seem like the type to hold hands. It shocked me how he could go from fucking me like he hated me to holding my hand like we were teenagers in love.

"I've got a surprise for you at home," he said matter-of-factly.

I wasn't sure I wanted any surprise he'd give. I started to fear arriving at my house. What would I walk into?

"Why are you being weirdly nice? I want the man that's going to fuck me like I'm nothing more than a whore."

He stopped walking, grabbing my arm with his free hand and making me face him. He moved that hand to palm my cheek, his thumb caressing below my eye. I closed my eyes, mesmerized by his gentle touch. I felt his hand tear away from my face, and instead, he squeezed the side of my throat at the base.

"I can be nice to you because I treated you like shit and

punished you for something you didn't do while still fucking you like you're my personal whore, because you are," he said, whispering in my ear. He licked from the base of my neck to below my ear, then nibbled on the lobe. "And trust me, my surprise isn't traditional," he promised.

A devilish smirk took over his face before he let go of my throat, and we continued the short walk to my place.

Tonight, I was thankful that I had private housing off campus. When my stalker—now known as Killian—first arrived, Briar and Dex wanted me to move in with them. I told them I'd be okay alone, even as he progressively got closer. I killed men before, so I wouldn't cower from one. Preston tried to get me to move, too, but I refused to be run out of my own home.

I went to unlock my front door when we arrived, but it was already unlocked, though it was still dark inside. I flipped on the living room light.

"You can take off that hoodie now. We're alone," he advised.

It was cold on the way here, so at least it served a purpose beyond hiding my body. I chucked it off and threw it to the ground. Killian's eyes immediately wandered my body.

"Fuck. My work is so beautiful. You're so beautiful," he said.

He closed the gap between us and stalked toward me, his fingers grabbing the hem of my skirt and pulling me flush against him.

"You're insatiable," I teased with a giggle.

"With you? Yes. I could fuck you every hour of the day, and it still wouldn't satisfy me. I need you more than I need air. I've got a lot of lost time to make up for, darling. That starts now."

"Good. Don't let me go, Killian. I need you, too. You're the only one who will ever be able to give me exactly what I need," I said.

"Run, doll. When I get my hands on you, I will ravish you," he advised.

It took me a minute to take in his words, but when I did, I darted up the stairs. My house wasn't that big, and there weren't many places to hide. He'd find me reasonably quickly, which excited me. He was giving me what I asked for without judgment. I'd kill his father again for taking this time away from us if I could.

My room was dark; of course, he knew which room it was, but I decided to head for that door. I shut the door behind me and went into my closet, which was extremely dark. I held onto my mouth to keep from breathing too loud.

I heard his footsteps running up the stairs.

"I'm coming for you, Aster. I can't wait to find you. You're too obvious," he said.

His voice seemed close, and I guessed he was outside my door. I heard it open, and his footsteps entered my room, and then the light flickered on. I wasn't alone in the closet when my eyes opened from the intrusion.

I let out a blood-curdling scream when I noticed Preston there, tied up, gagged, and bloody.

Aster

"**A**h, good, you've found my present," Killian said with a wicked grin when he opened the door.

I jumped out of the closet. "What the fuck is he doing in my closet?" I screamed.

Killian didn't answer. Instead, he walked to my bedside, grabbed a box with a bow, and presented it to me. "Here. There's more."

I wasn't sure I wanted to open the box, but against my better judgment, I did. I sighed at the sight. Thankfully, I wasn't squeamish. "Fingers?" There were two of Preston's fingers in the box, which explained some of the blood.

Killian came up behind me and placed his hands on my hips, pulling me close. "For touching you. I said I'd cut off the fingers of any man that touched you the wrong way. What he did constitutes wrong. I should've cut out his tongue for how he spoke to you, but then I wouldn't be able to cum to his pleas when I fuck you in front of him."

Killian walked over to the closet and pulled the gag off of Preston.

"You son of a bitch, don't fucking touch her!" Preston yelled. Little did he know, I wanted Killian to touch me, and I loved that Preston would be watching. I wanted Preston to know how little he meant to me. How he never truly satisfied me; he only made me feel ashamed.

Killian stalked toward me, pushing my front half down on the bed so my ass was in the air while my chest was on the bed. I gripped the blanket, holding it tight, preparing to be ravished like he promised.

"I'm going to do more than just touch her, Pretty Boy." His voice was hoarse and commanding as he wedged his knee between my legs and pushed them apart.

He hiked my skirt up around my waist and smacked my ass. Preston tried to shimmy in the tape and ropes that bound him, but he hardly moved.

Killian's fingers trailed down my ass and rubbed the wetness accumulating in my slit. I moaned. One touch and I was melting like putty in his hands.

"Fuuuuck, my wet little slut is already ready for me," he groaned.

He backed away from my exposed body, and I felt empty without him there. When I turned to the side, he brandished a knife in Preston's face, kneeling down to his seated height.

"You're going to watch me fuck her like you should have. Frankly, I'm glad you didn't, or we wouldn't be in this position. If you look away, I'll gouge out your eyes, Pretty Boy," he threatened, running the blade's sharp edge down his cheek and cutting.

He walked back toward me, the knife put away but cuffs in his hand. He cuffed my wrists together, then pulled out a restraint rope from under my bed, which hooked to the cuffs. I had no idea this was there. I didn't know when he had it installed. The rope reached me across the bed, snuggly holding me in place.

The position wasn't exactly comfortable, but I didn't want

comfort. I wanted the pain. Because of Killian, I'd never be able to have regular sex again. I'd need the pain, mask, or chase to get off. Much like I suspected he did, too.

I tugged my arms on the ropes as a test, but I hardly budged.

"Keep trying, love. Nothing's getting you out of there." He stood in front of me, watching me struggle. I smirked at him before he walked around the bed and stood behind me again. I heard the zipper of his pants come undone and then heard them drop to the floor. I couldn't turn my head easily to see what was happening, but I grew suspicious when I didn't feel him enter me.

Instead, I felt the flat of his tongue pressing on my clit before moving downward and lapping up my wetness from my slit. Then, his tongue plunged inside of me, and I moaned. I watched as Preston tried to turn his head away. He could read the pleasure on my face. His face blanched, and his lips curled in disgust.

I felt empty when his tongue left my pussy. I groaned.

"Don't worry, doll. I'll fill you again soon. See what you missed out on, Preston? Wait until you see her face when she orgasms. It's a beautiful sight," Killian teased.

"I've seen it before," Preston gritted out.

"I mean when she really orgasms, not when she's faking it," Killian said before slamming into me so hard that the bed shook, and I moved forward in the restraints, tugging harshly on them.

He was right, too. It was never real with Preston. I didn't even know sex could feel so good before tonight.

Killian reached forward and roughly grabbed my hair, pushing my cheek into the mattress.

"Fuck. You should feel how wet she's getting just from me slamming into her," Killian bragged. "Should I show Preston how you loved to be fucked in the ass by your stepbrother?" I wish I felt embarrassed at his humiliation and degradation, but I didn't.

"No. Please don't," I pleaded. I meant it this time. I was already torn apart back there and suffering from the aftereffects.

"The sound of your begging makes me so fucking hard, darling," Killian whispered near my ear before he bit the back of my neck, sucking the spot and surely leaving a mark. His mark. He wanted to show he owned me to Preston and the world. "I'm one lucky man, Preston. She wore no underwear for you, but then I showed up instead. I took her in that bathroom, against the sink and the door, while she thought I was you."

"You son of a bitch. Stop touching her; she doesn't want it!" Preston shouted.

Killian pulled my hair up, forcing me to look at Preston. My eyes were wide and full of tears from Killian using me at his mercy. My pussy was already painfully brutalized all night, and I wasn't sure it could take much more. It still felt good. I liked the pain.

"Tell him if you want me to stop," Killian directed.

I shook my head. "No. Please don't stop. It feels good," I answered.

He let go of my hair and let my head fall down to the bed. Then, he smacked my ass a few times until I was sure it was red.

"That's the problem, Preston. I give her what she wants. I see the dark side of her and oblige to her whims. You didn't. You would've never been enough because I left a stain on her soul when I met her."

I heard the flick of a knife that I wasn't sure how Killian got his hands on. He reached below me and squeezed my neck, pulling my head up again and forcing me to look at Preston. His thrusts were at a brutal pace and strength, pushing my hips repeatedly into the side of the bed. I felt the cold steel of the knife caress my cheek. The angle of his thrusts caused him to hit a deep spot inside of me that had my vision darkening and my moans becoming louder. I didn't even need him to touch my clit because it kept pressing up against the bed with each thrust. Because of the restraints, my body couldn't be flush against his, but I wished it could.

"Once I'm untied, I'm going to fucking kill you," Preston promised with darkened eyes.

"Bold of you to assume you'll ever be out of them," Killian responded. "Or that you can kill me when you're missing two fingers on your dominant hand." I heard Killian chuckle.

Killian

After I cut into her cheek, I brought the blade to my tongue and cleaned it off with my tongue.

"Delicious," I said, winking at Preston.

"You're sick," he spat.

"You haven't even seen the worst of me," I responded.

I lifted Aster's hips slightly to thrust into her at the perfect angle. I kept my thrusts hard, deep, and rhythmic. I set the knife down on the bed, holding my other hand lightly on her throat. My other hand traveled under her lingerie top to her chest, pinching one of her nipples hard. I squeezed and twisted while she cried out, tears streaming down her face—a beautiful sight.

"I want to feel you come around my cock," I told her, my hand squeezing her throat tighter on the sides, restricting her breathing. She was already a garbled mess but couldn't speak or breathe now. I loved being the one to make her that way. When I felt her body on the verge of becoming limp, I let go, letting her fall to the bed and catch her breath.

"You're such a good girl for me, Aster," I cooed.

"Killian," she said breathily before letting out a string of unintelligible curses as her thighs began to shake. I slowed down my thrusts as her walls started to clench me. It took everything inside me not to come right then and there. Being inside her felt fucking amazing—so wet, warm, and tight. Suddenly, I wanted to gouge Preston's eyes out for even seeing my girl like this, even though I was the one who made him watch.

He wouldn't be alive later anyway, so it wasn't like he needed his eyes.

"Jesus fucking Christ, Killian," she moaned, burying her head in the bed.

I kept my slow pace but made sure to hit her deep inside. I wanted to make sure her body never forgot mine. Never forgot who she belonged to. "You feel so good inside me."

"Look him in the eye and show him what he missed out on. He'll know I'm the only one that makes you feel this way, doll."

"Look at what you'll never have again, Preston," she said. "Look at how good he fucks me and how incredible he makes me feel. You were nothing compared to him."

Preston wrestled against his ropes, but his eyes remained on her. His lips were tight while he watched, but his dick was growing in his pants. He enjoyed watching my girl get off, even if it was by another man, and he'd pay for that later.

Once the shaking subsided, I kneeled behind her. I leaned forward, pressing my tongue on her clit a few times before moving back toward her slit. My tongue entered her, her thighs smashing my head as I smirked against her pussy. I devoured her like my favorite meal. The sweet taste of her was something I'd savor for the rest of my damn life.

"Killian, please. It's so sensitive," she pleaded.

I didn't let up. I gave her a few harsh tongue thrusts as she tried to wiggle away from me, then I pulled out. I moved my tongue up and between her cheeks, licking the puckered hole. I smirked when she tried to get out of my grip. I slapped her ass for even trying, but I pulled away and stood up again.

I pushed back inside her with ease, thrusting to the hilt immediately.

"You know the best part, Preston?" He didn't answer. The guy looked like he was about to murder me with his mind. If he could, he would. "I fucked her so much tonight that washing her couldn't free her from being filled with my cum. Now, I get to use it as lube. Push it deeper inside of her. You know what that means, right?"

His eyes widened. Now I got him talking. "She's not on birth control. She—she let you inside without a condom?" I wasn't sure she even knew what she was doing this entire night. I don't think the thought ever occurred to her.

I pushed into her harder again, pushing her cheek into the bed to anchor myself as I thrust like a madman into the woman I hunted down for the past year. "She doesn't *let* me do anything."

I picked up the knife again and ran the flat of the blade down her spine. "So beautiful," I said. I trailed it down to her lower back and stopped above her ass, nicking the skin and watching the blood fall to the bed. "I love watching you bleed and being the one to make you bleed."

"I want you to cum inside me, Killian. So deep inside me. I want to hurt when I sit down, and I want to be so full of you," Aster begged. I waited years to hear her say those words. Fuck, they sounded good coming from her mouth.

"Your wish is my command, darling." I smacked her ass, then stilled while deep inside her, shooting ropes of cum inside of her while she made herself clench my cock. I moaned as I released more cum than I ever had in my life, making my final claim on the woman I had obsessed over for years. Now that I had her, I wasn't letting go. No one would stop me—especially not Pretty

Boy Preston.

I pulled up my pants and boxers when I finally pulled myself away from her. I got on the bed and uncuffed her from the restraint system. Then, I pulled her skirt down since she could not move at the moment. She looked spent.

I moved the sweaty hair from her face and kissed her cheek. "You did so good, love. Don't worry about moving for now. I've got this."

I approached Preston with my knife in hand. He tried to scoot backward while I stood before him, but he only ended up falling over. I sat on top of him, facing him while using my knee to hold his stomach down. He wiggled beneath me, but my knee held too tight for anything to happen.

"Want to know what happens when you touch what's mine?" I asked with a sadistic grin.

He shook his head like a pussy. I rolled my eyes, tired of him. Playing with my food was getting boring.

I braced my knife and shoved it into the side of his neck twice. He gargled blood as it pooled out of his new stab wounds. I removed the knife to watch the bright red substance leak onto the floor. Watching him lose blood rapidly while dying before me was enough to make me hard again. He blinked, and I knew he was too alive for me. I brought my knife up and smashed it into his chest harshly before removing it.

I folded it again and shoved it into my pocket. Preston's lifeless body remained on her floor while I stood up and walked back to her. I wiped the flat end of the blade down her arm, trailing his blood. I loved to see her in blood, especially of someone we killed.

I lifted her from the bed, bringing her face-to-face with me. I palmed her cheek in my hands, looking into her desolate eyes.

"You killed him," she said.

"Are you disappointed?" I asked, tilting my head and searching her face for answers. Would she hate me for what I did?

She shook her head. "Only that I didn't get to be the one to do it," she responded.

I grinned. There's my girl. The murderous psychopath who belonged to me.

"I wanted to kill that fucker for you. You were too tired, and I was too tired of him being alive. Don't worry. I'll let you do it the next time you get the murderous itch. Okay?" I kissed the top of her head, and she smiled at me.

"What now?" she asked.

"We burn this fucking place down and start fresh. I believe we have one more person to take care of."

I brought her face to mine and smashed our lips together hungrily, bringing her in for a desperate kiss. Killing turned me on, and watching me kill turned her on. But we had work to do on this place.

"What about when they come looking for him? I was his girlfriend."

"Don't worry, I took care of it," I assured her.

"How did you even do all of this tonight? It was like you were in two places at once."

I smiled. "Because I didn't do it alone." I winked at her. She'd never meet my hired accomplice, though.

Aster

Two Months Later

Killian was right. He took care of everything that Halloween night. He sent fake texts while in the room with Preston, detailing to his friends and family how he would hurt me. So when his remains were found burned in my apartment, I had an alibi, and Preston had a motive. He, according to police, set fire to my place but got caught in it. I should've felt sad witnessing his death and probably shouldn't have been happily fucking his killer, except Preston was nothing to me compared to Killian. He was someone to kill the time with; then, he became an abusive cheater.

Killian and I got a short-term rental for the school year, and then we planned on moving to Boston to join Briar. Briar was ecstatic to know I'd remain in her life. She was, however, curious about me fucking my former stepbrother. She wasn't judgmental, though, and that's when I fully decided to move for her. She was my best friend. She never once even questioned anything about Preston. According to her and Dex, we went back to watch a movie with them and fell asleep on their couch.

Briar was my ride-or-die. No friendship would ever compare.

"Are you ready for this?" Killian asked as we sat outside his childhood home—the home my mother and I moved into.

I nodded and took his hand in mine, walking in together. I still had a key.

"What the fuck are you doing here?" my mother asked when we approached her in the living room. She was seated on the couch, smoking a cigarette and drinking a bottle of vodka.

"Putting an end to your lies," I answered.

"You wanted me to kill her. You set her up to die, and for what?" Killian questioned.

My mother snickered. "That little bitch ran around tempting him, then killed him when he did what was natural. All he did was care for us. Then, he dared to leave everything to her. I was the one who married the fucker and willingly sucked his old dick," she spewed.

"She was a teenager, you miserable fuck."

"I warned her about men early on! It's her fault. She didn't listen; she never did."

"Here's the thing, *Mom*," I said. "I let you live in this house because I wanted nothing more than to run away. But, you see, I own the house and everything in it. Your pedophile husband left it all to me. So, you're going to get the fuck out," I advised, flicking out my pocket knife that I held tightly in my hand, "Or I'm going to kill you." I presented her options with a sadistic grin on my face.

"You wouldn't. I'm your mother. Where would I go?"

"Oh, I would. Giving birth to me doesn't mean shit when you always put yourself first. I would've been better off without you. In fact, maybe I should take care of that burden now and do it anyway."

My mother jumped from her seat and started walking toward the front door. "Where am I supposed to go?" Her pleas were beyond pathetic. Did she think she'd convince me to give a fuck about her when she didn't care about me? She put her husband above me for two years. A man she hardly knew when she forced me to live with him.

I laughed. "Why do I fucking care? Go back to the club or something. Maybe they'll take your old ass back as a custodian."

Killian opened his wallet and threw a few hundred dollars at her. "Here. Take this and get the fuck out of my sight before I kill you myself, Carol." I wished he would so I'd never have to see her face again, but he said we needed to keep a low profile for now. People couldn't keep dying around us.

She ran out the door with nothing but her purse and shoes.

"Mmm, so what do we do now?" I asked, wrapping my arms around my boyfriend and bringing him into a hug. It felt odd to be back in the home I spent my high school years in, but being here with him felt right. We were robbed of so much that we were starting to get back.

"I have a buyer for the house. Now, we take the money from the sale and get us a house together in Boston after you graduate," he responded.

"Oh my God. Aster!" A female voice called behind me.

I turned around to see the source: Sarah, a housemaid I hadn't seen since I left.

"Sarah!" I ran toward her and brought her into a hug.

"You've returned and brought Killian."

"Hi, Sarah. We were evicting Aster's mother," Killian explained.

"Oh, thank God. She was awful. Are you two living with us again?" she beamed.

"No. We're moving to Boston after I finish my last semester of school. We, uh, we're...pregnant," I said. I wasn't sure how the maids would respond since they knew us when we lived together as siblings, even if we never felt that way.

"I'm so happy for you," she responded with a genuine smile.

"Hey, Sarah. Take this card and take all the staff out for lunch. I need the house to myself for a few hours," Killian said, handing her a credit card.

Sarah blushed. Killian couldn't have been more obvious.

"Just remember we can clean up any mess."

Killian

"You really didn't have to do that, Kill," Aster said once the maids left.

I smirked, stepping closer toward her.

"Yes, I did. I want to do what I should've done all those years ago, Aster. I want to fuck you in this house. And I don't want any disruptions. I want you to scream my name in this house. Then, we're going to leave this place behind," I told her.

I walked toward her while she stepped backward until her back pressed against a wall. I leaned into her, placing my palms on the wall on either side of her head and boxing her in. I smirked down at her.

"Now I've got you all to myself," I told her, leaning in and kissing from her jawline to the base of her neck. I bit into her neck, sucking on the skin and licking it to soothe the bruise I planned to leave.

"As long as you don't go soft on me just because I'm pregnant," Aster mumbled lustfully, her head tilted to the side to give me better access while I kissed, bit, and sucked on the side of her neck.

I chuckled. "I'll never go soft on you, doll. Don't worry your pretty little head. But we are going to try something new."

She wiggled her brows. I wedged my knee between her thighs,

and she rubbed on my thigh with her clothed pussy. There were too many layers of clothing between us. I wasn't going to take her here against this wall, though. No matter how good she looked or how sweet she smelled.

"Run upstairs, doll," I told her.

I stood back, releasing her from the box I put her in and allowing her to run away as directed. She looked at me momentarily before running and dashing up the stairs. I gave her a moment so I could get prepared. I went through the luggage I had left by the door, looking for the toy I had buried in my clothing to keep her eyes away.

"I'm coming," I called up the stairs as I began to take them two at a time. I'd never get sick of chasing her down. And once our child was born, I'd do it more aggressively again. For now, I didn't want to throw her to the ground and risk injuring our child. I could still hurt her without harming the pregnancy, though. I promised her I wouldn't treat her too differently. I'd never be the kind of guy Preston was—boring, dull, and cute. None of those words described me.

I first decided to look in my old room, but she wasn't there. I went to her old room, and the door was open. She was on the bed, naked. I groaned when I looked at her, my dick jumping in my pants and straining in my jeans.

"This is how I should've taken you. In your room the moment I met you. I should've claimed you so my father and everyone knew you were mine."

"This is the bed where your father told me he'd take my virginity on my eighteenth birthday," she said flatly. "I want to replace that memory with his son fucking me into oblivion on the same bed. He never got to have me, but you do."

She didn't have to tell me twice. I threw off my shirt quickly, and my jeans and boxers followed while I let them fall to the ground before stepping out of them. I grabbed my toy from my pocket before approaching the bed, where she lay on her back, propped up on her elbows.

"I brought a present," I told her, waving the vibrator and winking.

"What's that?" she asked.

I smirked and crawled on the bed. I brought myself between her legs, placing my arms under her thighs and pulling her toward me. I inhaled the scent of her sweet pussy before diving in, flicking her clit rhythmically with my tongue. Her thighs squeezed my head while she tried to squirm away from me, but I pulled her toward her more, burying my face against her bare pussy.

"Oh, fuck, Killian," she moaned. She previously told me the hormones make everything more intense. That was why I decided to bring a toy into the picture finally.

I speared her on my tongue as her back arched off the bed, greedily pushing her more into my face instead of trying to squirm away. I hummed my approval, and she exploded like a firework into my mouth. I lapped up her juices until she was done, then sat up and grabbed the toy.

"This is a vibrator. It curves so it's on your clit while also inside you, and then I slip in, too. It's supposed to be amazing."

When it started to buzz, her eyes widened. I twisted it to the correct angle and then placed it inside her. She moaned and tried to squirm away, but she wouldn't escape the vibrations.

I grabbed her legs, sat on my knees, and placed her feet over my shoulder. Thankfully, she was wet as fuck. I'd need the wetness to fit with the vibrator. She struggled with my size alone. I inserted two fingers into her and thrust a few times to help prepare her. Then, I replaced my fingers with the head of my cock and started to push inside.

The vibrations strumming along my cock felt fucking incredible. Holy shit. It would take everything in me not to come immediately. I pushed inside her slowly while her body stretched to fit me.

She propped herself on her elbows and looked down, watching where our bodies connected.

"See how beautifully your pussy swallows my cock, love? I knew you could do it. You're doing so fucking good." I could tell she liked what I said when her walls briefly clenched around me.

"The vibrations...they're too much," she said, lying on her back again. Her hips arched off the bed, driving me deeper into her. "Please, move. Hard. I need it."

I pulled back out before sinking back inside her, deeper than before. The vibrations felt so good that I wanted to stop, but I wanted to give my girl what she wanted. And I loved hearing her beg for it.

"Beg harder," I said, slowly picking up my pace but keeping my thrusts shallow.

"Fuck me, Killian. Please. Hard and rough. Please hurt me. You're driving me insane."

I smiled. My next thrust into her was so hard and deep that she moved up on the bed, and the headboard made a loud sound when it hit the hall. Her hands rested on my thigh, her nails digging into the skin. I leaned forward more, wrapping a hand around her throat and squeezing the sides, but not enough to constrict her breathing.

"Fuck, Aster. You're so fucking beautiful with my hand as a necklace, baby. And you're so fucking tight with this vibrator. I can't wait to feel you come on my cock," I told her.

"Oh, God," she moaned, her hands grabbing my wrist and squeezing while I tightly held her throat.

"There's no God here. Just the devil, ready and willing to sin for you," I reminded her.

"Oh Christ, that feels so fucking good," she moaned between garbled curses. "I'm coming, babe. Holy shit, I'm coming."

I watched as her eyes rolled to the back of her head, and she screamed my name, her body convulsing underneath mine.

"Seeing stars yet, baby?" I asked her with a grin. I knew we'd both enjoy the toy. I could already feel my balls tightening, ready to burst.

I let go of her throat, placing both hands on her breasts and squeezing her nipples. My girl loved the pain in any form. I loved to hurt her, but only when it pleased her.

"I knew when I met you that I'd never be able to let you go. You're fucking *mine*. Always," I growled.

I stilled deep inside her, dropping her legs to the bed and leaning forward to bury my face in her neck. I moaned into her neck while my cock throbbed inside of her, which was indistinguishable from the intense vibrations.

"I love when you fill me with your cum, baby. Give me every last drop," Aster encouraged.

I bit into her neck while she cried out, her pleas only making me come so fucking hard my vision blurred.

"Oh God, please make this thing stop, Killian. I—I can't take it anymore," she begged with a shaky voice, her breathing increasing again.

I smirked. "Oh, you think we're done? I don't think you've orgasmed enough. Now, flip over. Onto your hands and knees, doll."

Once would never be enough with Aster.

About the Author

Ashley is a debut author living in Nashville, TN, with her fiancé, three guinea pigs, and a bunny. When she's not writing or reading, she's probably photographing a concert or playing a video game. She enjoys reading dark romance, contemporary romance, and romantasy. TikTok: ashleyreyesphoto

You can connect with me on:
🌐 https://ashleyreyesauthor.com

Subscribe to my newsletter:
✉ https://mailchi.mp/880c58432bd1/5vq3e3h0pw

Made in the USA
Monee, IL
29 October 2024

68944278R00059